LAMENTING SORES

Shivi Pandey

Published by InkQuills Publishing House
www.inkquills.in

First Edition 2019
All Rights Reserved. Copyright © 2019

ISBN: 978-81-939985-1-9

DEDICATED TO

The Girl Who Solicited Forever

CONTENT

A MOMENT

Just need a moment,

To relax and ponder over the detriment,

In order to correct and implement...

No time to waste,

Everyone is in haste,

People do not believe in rest...

Some moments to think,

And write it down with the ink,

Maybe, then blink...

Some moments of golden sunshine basking,

Some desires still asking,

I am unaccomplished, please carry tasking...

Some moments to express love,

Like the calm and peaceful dove,

I plead to life, carry me, put me in a cove...

Some moments of success,

After an amass mess,

I covet nothing more than to win the race…

Some moments of glory,

After a long and tedious story,

And I solicit the hurt people a sorry…

Some moments to rest in peace,

And the rest to cease,

To be completely at ease…

Some moments of leisure,

To access pleasure,

I fetch in myself, the buried treasure…

Some moments of power,

To cherish and flower,

To prevent being a cower.

BATTLES

Zero and one,

Hundreds and none,

How many battle has anyone won?

Millions to quantify,

as said, nothing to specify,

What is it that you want to rectify?

Counts infinite,

Regardless of the might,

Galloping and swallowing the soul just as termite.

Self, the residence,

turmoil within, the evidence,

cosmic holocaust of nonsense.

Feeding on the belief as a leech,

Every now and then there is this itch,

as the wound was never stitched,

is something that disturbs each.

How many battles has anyone won?

Some hundreds and some none,

Failure or triumph, for many they are just done.

BLUE MOUNTAIN

Blue mountain,

Black river,

Little soul under tremor.

Black soil,

Red leaves,

Mortality thieves.

Decomposed unearthed,

Parasite breeding,

Hell succeeding.

Howling winds,

Dark moon,

Death coming soon.

SHIVI PANDEY

BROKEN PIECES

Broken pieces, loose hinges,

Unwanted inmates, silent shrugs,

Unclaimed integrity, vulnerable promises,

Erratic tenure, lengthy accusations,

Misguided supposition, misinterpreted
articulation,

Bewildered mind, victimized heart,

Succumbed feelings, hammered past,

Shredded leaves, scornful grievances,

Ruthless motives, humble patience,

Unaccountable nepotism, incongruous
narcissism,

Starving aspirations, underdog present,

Umpteenth hope, jeopardized life.

COGNIZANCE

Everything is inside you and you never know what just pops out of the toaster out of a sudden. Sometimes you feel it is just imagination and sometimes you feel you always had that niche in you and sometimes it is more of a déjà-vu.

Either it is on or off. Either it is zero or one. Either it exists or it doesn't. But how can something exist if it is not there. Or if it was already there why it pops out abruptly; Why does it feel dormant and void often. What is the illusion actually that is being talked about? Is absence the illusion or the presence?

Are you real or it is just what I choose to see?

Does the mind penalize the eyes to show me what it wants to feel or the eye blurs the mind to understand what it shows?

Are we self or just another molecular structure out of some random nebula with the same elementary composition?

Why do we have questions and how do we actually ask "why".

Are we making efforts good enough to learn the universe or is the cognizance crafted by the creator itself?

COMPILATION OF MY VULNERABILITY

When I felt love I was a baby and didn't even speak. Whenever I cried someone fed me, whenever I felt sleepy someone just rocked me to sleep and whenever I felt wet someone just changed my diapers. That was my first love!!

When I felt lonely someone used to listen to me. When I was afraid someone embraced me and whenever I was disappointed someone was there to cheer me up. She was my first friend, my sister. That was my second love!!

Then one day my second love left me for another man and my first love left for the heavenly abode.

Then I found her. My loneliness vanished and I overcame fear. She always cheered me up no matter what. I felt love again.

Then one fine day I discovered lust too and it felt like love adulterated. It felt wrong and sinned. It originated from within and I felt guilty. This love was different and poisoned and I felt helpless as I could not get rid of it. I wanted only love like the first and second. I confessed my love to her, maybe love and lust to her and she left.

I felt lonely, disappointed and afraid. I waited for her to return but she never returned. She did not feel love.

I felt even more lonely and afraid. I was neither dead nor alive. Trapped somewhere in between I developed anxiety. A curse that doesn't let you live nor let you die.

I experience it every day. I carry it and feed it but I am unable to surpass it. It is me and I am it. This is my real love which never let me sleep neither be awake. Not sad not happy. It never leaves me alone.

Anxiety and I congratulations!!!

SHIVI PANDEY

EMOTIONS

Emotions arise but I kill it,

Passion excites but I suppress it,

Heart pumps faster and I succumb to it.

Piston thrusts the blood but I consume it,

Sensation erupts but I cage it,

The fire burns but I diffuse it.

The dramatic dilemma occurs but I blow it,

The heart and the mind quarrel but I hoax it,

The burglars hide within me but I alibi it.

Something governs me to decide so I decide it,

Something allures me to be malleable so I follow it,

Something urges me to write so I write it.

FILTER

Is it filtered?

Doubtful? Wait a minute,

What do you see now?

I see beyond the smiles,

I see beyond the lies,

I see beyond the deceit.

Oh! So does this lens really work?

Or is it just a vivid illustration of myth,

Or is it some kind of truth bandwidth filter?

Wait... let me zoom in a bit,

I see concave lips beyond smiles,

I see the horrifying truth beyond lies,

I see hurt and hatred beyond deceit.

That's great but I never saw such perspicuously,

How do you see it?

Is it some additional feature?

No dear, actually it is just the filter that I removed.

The unfiltered images are much more lucid,

And the zoom in gives details with such clarity I fail to comprehend.

I HAVE A FRAME

I have a frame with lot of faces but I recognize only one,

Never met but feels more than just someone.

When loneliness engulfs I swallow a lump,

Deaf and dumb yet the heart connects and it's numb.

Memories not much as of yet,

But not such that I regret.

Together is happiness,

Close or distanced it is never any less.

Forever is an illusion without you, Forever is you.

SHIVI PANDEY

NO URGES NO PAIN

I hold no urges and no pain,

I don't care if I lose or gain,

What I crave is just company,

For, it is not available to many.

Lost my heart and soul and the mind was looted
of lively thoughts,

I tried to complete sentences but found myself
struggling to connect the dots.

You came like the monsoon shower,

And you left flooding me forever,

A memory that I cherish even today,

I am afraid with time it shall decay,

What decays not is the story,

Which even being true will be served as myth and
misery,

Promises seem to be wary,

As now even sorry is not enough to carry.

IDEAS WITHIN INVERTED COMMA

World is the desire and you are a dream,
Desire is true but dream is a lie.

Love is optional but lust is mandatory,
Companionship is hobby and lust is survival.

Love is abstract while lust is tangible,
Madness is illusion while money is real.

Relationship is fear and power the security,
family is burden and wealth the aid.

#MessedUp!!!

IN GRIEF

See, I will tell you in brief,

Let me tell you about grief,

It is not only the outcome of some random mischief.

Sometimes or let us consider many a time,

We consider our actions to be the prime,

But it is rather outsourced and none can define.

When grief rejoices,

Whom do you trust, your faiths or choices?

I know mind is full of chaotic voices.

Nevertheless, choice is your faith,

And to keep faith is only your choice,

So when in grief, just repeat: it is the outcome of some causal mischief.

So when in grief, Only self-belief, Is the ultimate relief.

PROTECT

In order to protect themselves people lived in caves, made weapons, built mud houses, fenced it then they cleared the forest, made strong walls and henceforth started living in towns and cities away from the forest.

Now people in order to protect themselves from modern day monsters search for haven to get liberated or they leave behind the materialistic things in order to find the true meaning of life into the deep solitude of the forests or mountains. What they are not aware of is the fact that unknowingly they are surrendering their lives to some more diabolical monsters or to the animal kingdom where life itself hold no meaning.

Beware! Do not step into the ambiguous premise looking for answers to liberate yourself.

SHIVI PANDEY

IN THE SILENCE OF THE NIGHT

In the silence of the night,

When all things are dull and nothing seems right,

I remember the morning will be bright.

In the instigating hollow,

When life seems crippled and shallow,

I chant something that I follow,

In the darkness's premise,

After the shadow's demise,

It's only me now, to be precise.

In the undefined sorrow,

Each minute that I borrow,

I promise to payback tomorrow.

In the silence of the night,

When all things are dull and nothing seems right,

LAMENTING SORES

I choose the unthreaded kite.

In the silence of the night when I serve as the
guiding light...

SHIVI PANDEY

IN THE SPACE CALLED ECSTASY

In the space called ecstasy,

There's this delicacy,

Moreover, prophesy.

A prophesy that I declare,

One day we shall share,

Each moment and that too everywhere.

Moment shall not define,

The time, that sublime,

But only love, perfectly divine.

Divine is the destiny,

And its mystic ways to scrutiny,

Backfired like mutiny.

In the space called ecstasy,

Much is fantasy,

Left over is fallacy.

IT HAS BEEN A LONG TIME

It has been a long time,

Reminded the wind chime,

And as I sip through my water, lime

The music in silence, so sublime,

 Brought back the duo time,

When your prayers echoed like rhyme.

It has been a long time,

When we moved out at nine,

At a nearby restaurant to dine,

For the dish-utmost prime,

Garnished with delicate enzyme,

 Satisfying the taste buds with you, just felt divine.

It has been a long time,

When lame jokes of mine,

Never annoyed you, my sunshine,

And all night we drank on a bottle of wine,

Discussing the life together, it was really great and fine,

Only then my lonely house felt more like a shrine.

It has been a long time,

Since I saw your last smile,

As you left for the west but feels just like a mile,

For the dinner table still counts nine,

And there is lot of unfinished wine,

You see, then and now life hasn't moved an inch in time.

It has been a long, really long time...

JUDGE

Yesterday, it felt like I had the best life possible. There was passion, there was zeal and most of all there was purpose of being. It all made sense and all because I decided to open up for you. To let you in, to make you feel wanted and not dejected. I was someone who was optimistic even in tough times.

Pardon me if you feel I am judging you again. I thought you just liked being nurtured like everybody else does and just because of some mishap you were harsh on yourself. It was quite relatable so I just wanted you to feel free and just wanted you to let go off things that were not something that you could control. So I just wanted to help you out, yes I was protective about you and was also a bit possessive about you but it was just a humanely gesture. I would have done the same thing had it been anyone. I just didn't know that you had shut down yourself from the outside world so much that you couldn't even bother to acknowledge the love that I had for you.

I know there was no deal as such and it was never a deal after all. It was just a waste, feeling like to be with you, to look after you, to listen to you and never judge you on anything.

Repeating again that I am not judging, but you were ignorant, cold, selfish, arrogant and pathetic.

Today, it is such that you are the most beautiful and the worst nightmare of my life that I have ever had but you really will not be able to even understand what I say because no matter what I say "I am judging you".

Let me tell you something that you did. Tomorrow if somebody helps me out or tries to help me out just the way I tried out of good gesture and good intentions obviously, I would do the same with that person as you did with me. Cold, selfish, ignorant, arrogant and pathetic so that that person turns out to be just like me and yes, also just like you.

We both are at par now. I have also shut down myself from the outside world and don't worry because I am not playing the blame game now. I just feel sorry for the person I was before; I just hope nobody tries to help me out ever as I have become toxic just like you.

Remember you had said "Thank god, I am not in a relationship or else the guy would have been screwed".

Today I also say that "Thank god, I am not in a relationship or else the girl would have been screwed" just the difference here is that you at least had the liberty of saying it to me but I have no one even to say the punch lines to. As you somehow had a friend like me who just listened to your

nonsense without complaints and judgment but
you know people, they judge.

SHIVI PANDEY

LAST LOVE

I had loved once and it was faint on my heart,
though the memories remain it doesn't unearth.

I had loved twice and it was one level up for this
instance made me cry, when my heart swelled,
finally went dry.

I had loved thrice but it was more of a disguise,
since I never mentioned it, to be wise.

Last now or maybe just a variable, it was simply
unfazed and inevitable.

Last love, the only one with extortion, it
plundered each and every subtle portion.

Mismatched, tilted, crooked and wicked,
completely sick and dead.

Last love, not just first second and third, absurd,
overheard; curse word.

Last love, not below and merely above,
Please! I have had enough.

LEGITIMATE OR ILLEGITIMATE

I had no idea what was up next. All was just good and all was as planned. Not even in my skeptical thoughts had I wondered in that premise.

Yet, you see, I just took an entire road trip that too with a map.

Wow! Seems funny, déjà vu.

Was it a great time or a just an intangible deluge because for me it was the latter.

How often does it happen?

Anyone?

Once in a week, a month or maybe year

Umm… Should I take it as a no?

Well it happened to and with me, once in a lifetime.

Tell me, is having desire wrong?

I believed that if one has desire he/she's alive and if one's alive he/she's bound to have desires.

I also desired someone, and my desire was legitimate.

Everyone has it. Was I wrong to crave?

My craving was just like everyone else, normal.

But my craving said to me that "cravings are not selfish".

My craving was selfless, I just believed what you give is what you get.

My craving always talked to me, shared its grievances with life and why was it in pain, why it always felt anxious, why it always wanted to stay aloof and why it never wanted to be anybody's craving. But eventually it became my craving.

Not even in my skeptical thoughts had I wondered in that premise. I was just helping out someone's unfulfilled craving oblivious to the intangible deluge that was to follow.

I developed such a holistic and zealous craving and suddenly it was more important than my own life "selfless".

But my craving said to me that "cravings are not selfish".

Indeed, it was selfish because the craving was a byproduct of being humane and being humane means believing what you give is what you get. Isn't it?

Now where did this return component come from?

Therefore, wasn't my craving, my desire legitimate?

And what about "I believed that if one has desire he/she's alive and if one's alive he/she's bound to have desires."?

Tell me aren't your cravings getting fulfilled? How does it get accomplished?

Aren't yours legitimate or only the illegitimate cravings succeed?

Tell me, I need to know and I want to correct my line of action. I want to learn from my wrong doings as I may be on the other side of the grass and maybe the other side is greener.

LESS OBVIOUS

In the so called life,

Diabolical yet always a surprise,

I noticed the less obvious.

From the unavoidable charm,

I regarded the elegant soul,

Because I noticed the less obvious.

From the crooked ideas of yours,

I bent for the blissful smile,

As I noticed the less obvious.

From the dejection that you were,

I always found the craving of acceptance for it,

As I noticed the less obvious.

From all the warnings of the world,

My heart with all its might, pounded for your
warmth,

LAMENTING SORES

As I noticed the less obvious.

From the acceptance of your dejection,

To the rejection of my acceptance,

I never anticipated the less obvious.

SHIVI PANDEY

LETTER OF RESIGNATION

Today, I resign

From your premise

Yes; I finally do!

As being true is judgmental,

While you being irrational is spruced

For the soul you are,

Detachment is inevitable.

Sympathy was solicited,

I lend my ear and time

Whereas Love and care was the appeal,

And abandonment was rewarded.

Today, I resign

From your premise

Yes; I finally do!

Not for my reward,

Neither for my appeal,

But for my mistake to

Fetch tenderness in you.

LONELY ISLAND

I am lonely,

So prone to death,

So close to bathe,

In the pool of waste, solemnly!

I am no one to resist,

The mesmerizing feeling, the beauty,

Of highly astonishing quality,

Spares me nowhere to exist.

Death's shadow,

Echoing all around,

Swiftly circling round,

Alone I am the only fellow.

The cold blowing breeze,

The terror marching in my vein,

It's approaching closer with its cane,

Oh! God rescue me please.

NOT AGAIN

Not again shall I ever nurture,
To be the prey of your vulture,
Not again.

Not again shall I tickle,
To be at chaos and fickle,
Not again.

Not again shall I attend to your miseries,
Neither will I bend to support your stories,
Not again.

Not again shall I find peace,
But I promise, love for you will cease,
Not again.

Not again shall I crave,
Now, reluctantly digging my grave,
Not again.

LAMENTING SORES

Not again! All in vain!

Not again! So insane!

Not again!

I plead to myself, just this time, save me again!

SHIVI PANDEY

OH! CIGARETTE

Finely cut tobacco rolled in thin paper,

Why do I need your stroke?

It was better if prior to this I broke,

I would prefer to burn my lips by a taper.

Why this immense attraction?

When it slowly dilapidates,

My body parts,

Is it just to be in a coalition?

It is brutal,

I am really very gullible,

I am also malleable,

I am a fool that is the conclusion in total.

I need it in number

Although I am in dissension,

But it continues in session,

Then I feel drowsy and slumber.

LAMENTING SORES

I desperately need it in my closet,

About these things, I am cagey,

These deeds must be quiet and not noisy,

Because it spoils your image, I bet.

I don't want to smoke but my mind veers,

It is a very good psychological orator

And then it spins my head later,

So this way it tears.

SHIVI PANDEY

OH! GOD

I need someone so pure,

For my lamenting heart to cure,

In whose arms I feel complete and secure.

Someone to share pain,

A haven for all my sorrows to drain,

I gladly submit my inexplicable soul to her
inexpugnable rein.

Someone to exude love,

Like the calm and peaceful dove

Without her I am just a rove.

ON MY JOURNEY TO LOVE

Sometimes when you sit to write and pick up an idea such as love or anything within its circumference you feel like oh! Shit, not again. What am I going to write? Yes, that same old shit again within some pricey words and exhilarating combination of non-living things, creating a metaphor or personifying things, those hold no worth in your vicinity. Then comes such beautiful heart melting imagination which is obviously not true but it makes a tickle inside and it molests your heart and mind just like alcohol. You then go on your journey to love and you see things that belong to your wildest imagination.

Hello? Please come back. This is the reality not what you went through. The work of an artist is to fool you and guess what? you pay for it, your time. It a mess, a complete mockery of you and your situation because we artist make you believe your life is shit and what we create is bliss.

We are a Big Time Con. We con your Time.

SHIVI PANDEY

PILGRIMAGE

Lending uncertainties to one another,

There began the pilgrimage for tranquility.

However mundane the path,

Neither had any signs of wrath,

For the souls decimated together,

Incommodious, yet ready to wither.

Blatantly nurturing the essence,

while promulgating omnipresence.

Derivative being affection,

conducing to abolish dissembling.

And when the call was but made,

the other soul attempted to evade.

Failing to deliver the boundless,

abandoned the other mockingly clueless.

SELF IMPROVEMENT

Positivity/Negativity

If simply thought there can be only two ways a person can think in any possible circumstance, positive or negative. There are lot of factors that enhance the way a person feels and react.

Almost everybody has felt low, depressed and fatigued at some point of time in life but very few know that it is absolutely okay to feel like a looser sometime and due to this ignorance they eventually push themselves into deeper misery. This is analogous to overreacting as this act is not required.

There are basically two ways to think about this situation, either over-think or just don't think at all. These are the only two ways our minds work.

When you think, you are composed, peaceful, focused and happy.

When you over-think, you are restless, irritated, angry and unhappy and you land up into depression and anxiety but there is a way out. You can train your brain to fight against negativity.

When you have some happy memories you like to keep them intact, because you feel it is completely okay to stick to some good moments and when you have some bad memories you want to get rid of them, why?? Why is it not okay to have bad memories too?

Out of infinite ways you try, this is the most legitimate way to get rid of the negativity and pain that it carries. Acceptance is the key to a happy and prosperous life. You accept love but not hatred, you accept pleasure but not pain, accept success and not failure. Why can't you accept everything as it is?

Human race is in an intermittent process of acquiring knowledge. Love and hatred, pleasure and pain, success and failure all are just a part of it and if you are experiencing all of this, it means you are walking towards a beautiful destination (An unimaginably beautiful), so rise to the level of acceptance and pass on the message for this mesmerizing future awaits you without any guilt and regrets.

SOAKING IN THE TURBULENCE

Soaking in the turbulence

Submerged in the ocean of blood

I dwell in the flood

A flood not to be undermined

Wrath and might with the ultimatum

Perennial slander as its dictum

Intermittent solace

Prejudiced answers

Alleged self-worth

Humongous surcharge

Overpowering bi parley

Capitulating heart

Soaking in the turbulence

Submerged in the ocean of blood

I dwell in the flood

A flood unreasonably indignant

Poised to rip apart

All of what seems adored

Unfazed with the culpability

Diminishing even the dearth

Of what remains as equity

Soaking in the turbulence

Submerged in the ocean of blood

I dwell in the flood.

SOME PLACE ELSE

On the terrace beneath the night sky,

Just your shadow and I

Wander the stars and beyond

Silently delivering through the eyes

The exploration stories

Without any boundaries

Containing hidden promises

Of travelling further to infinity

Holding the intersection between us

Till we surpass infinity

Where the numbers end

Where the light fades

Where the forces become impotent

Where the stars collapse and matter ends

Where sense makes no sense

Where the souls meet, numbers start, light is born, forces just exist and not act, matter takes form and logic is only a feeling, on a voyage to someplace else.

STILL ALIVE

I don't know how long I will crib over you neither do I know if I will be out of this agony someday. What I only know is that I had never thought I could walk this far post disaster. I still don't know if how far I need to go. I only have some memories and experiences that are deep rooted into the fabrics of my soul and I believe you can never see that. What I intermittently go through is an unending process of reasoning and questioning and reasoning it out again. Temporarily the reasoning justifies my inquiries but I need another one each day to refrain from being upset about myself.

If you think I am a looser then that is only because you think that way, but not me, I am way more branched into fetching myself than anyone would ever consider.

What accompanies me is self-criticism. What I am against are my decisions, my choices, maybe even my worth. But no to mention that I have not given up to the critics as I counter attack by questioning my ambiguity that I have with my state of being alive.

I am still living. Although not as I should be. Although not like anybody else who excels in their life. Also not like anybody who meticulously balances every aspect of his life but I am still alive.

Although not like the melancholic fussed in alcohol, also not like the escapist giving up on the responsibilities but I am still alive.

What I am living is a confusion and utter chaos inside the heart and mind that seems like the random honking horns in the traffic. You never know which vehicle want to go which way, whether it is left or right or just straight. Is anyone being in hurry to reach somewhere or if someone has just out for a ride or if there's a critical emergency for some or if the horns are just out of frustration. It seems similar to the different aspects of the chaos inside me.

Once and for all even if I decide to forgive you dear, there is no way I can forgive myself for what I have done because if I do, I would repeat the same mistake of being kind and good to someone else and I would feel the same again. Since few things are so deep rooted that you will miserably fail to see and there I am still alive.

Still figuring out to make a decision of going right or left or straight before the signal goes green again as everything has consequences and decisions are something that would later be my own critic. But there I am still alive.

SHIVI PANDEY

STUDDED WITH JEWELS

Studded with jewels

There she withheld

My ease to breathe

And all I did was just freeze.

Sultry afternoon

Annoying breeze

Fluttering hair kissing your cheeks

I remained silent and watched like a geek.

Excited souls two

One for the tour

Other for the sore

That vaguely promised anything more

Near yet far

Far yet near

Supposed to be one

But always remained two

LAMENTING SORES

Myth revealed

Requested to feel

Just wanted my sore healed

She said "go and hug the dead" it might fill

Three evenings

Three nights

Three days

And all possible ways

Studded with jewels

There she withheld

My ease to breathe

And all she did was shake hands, turn around and leave.

Sultry afternoon

Annoying breeze

Water camouflaged with sweat

I remained silent and gazed till she took leave.

SHIVI PANDEY

TELL ME, WHAT WAS IT?

Tell me, what was it?

No, don't you dare fool me

For all this while I was quiet and may be lame

All on me for the blame

And all on you for the fame

Tell me, what was it?

No, don't you dare fool me

Make and break, make and break and remake

All for the namesake

Pity on you, such a fake

Tell me, what was it?

No, don't you dare fool me

Run, fall, cry and sympathize

All in all, completely jeopardize

I need my revenue subsidized.

LAMENTING SORES

Tell me, what was it?

No, don't you dare fool me

Why did you engulf me and set yourself free?

Why you and why me

You know what, just let it be

Tell me, what was it?

No, don't you dare fool me

You put yourself to the immoral use

But hey! Listen, I will not abuse

Because I am not the one to lose

Tell me, what was it?

No, don't you dare fool me

I have felt something transforming

And after rigorous brainstorming,

I have clarity on you, this morning

Don't tell me what it was

Neither do I wish to know

No, you cannot fool me

Because now I don't judge and assume

But I am just glorified by the character in you,
and it is shit!

THIS

This, this particular place was once peaceful and rivers of distilled love flowed like the only elixir in the world, crowded by poisonous snakes, hissing in the grass ready to spit venom in life which had no antidote.

This, this particular place was once filled with the laughter and cacophony of toddlers and infants who were just beginning to learn that the world is a fairy tale, oblivious, to the devil that disguised itself as society, waiting to pounce as they stood and walked the turf no more dependent for a finger.

This, this particular place was once smooth and luxurious without the materialistic luxuries and the mind thought none and the actions followed the heart as there was nothing to lose as all that came was plenty and unasked for.

This, this particular place was once so content as it complimented everything else it had as companions for life and all that it was felt like togetherness and complete.

This, this particular place was once a nothing and everything where nothing existed and everything happened. The magic, life felt like!!!

SHIVI PANDEY

UNCONTROLLABLE LUST

Uncontrollable lust,

I have put forward all my trust,

Never let my love rust

As for me you are a must.

I try to preclude,

But the body has already gobbled the food,

And the dogmas set by it are rude,

So I submit and conclude.

I am debilitated, but I am skeptic,

Why am I behaving lunatic?

Do I have the mind of a rustic?

Also my wounds have become septic.

Oh...! my malignant sore,

From the avid heart's core,

My impatient eyes pour,

LAMENTING SORES

To glance thy passion more and even more.

WHERE DO I FIND PEACE?

Where do I find peace?

In the early morning sunrise or in the delicacies of life,

In the world full of lies or in my closet where time flies.

In the sinful pleasure or in the smiles that can last forever,

In looking for an answer or living one.

In holding on to a judgment or dismissing some, unanswered

In putting forward "?" or simply returning "."

Can you tell me where peace resides???

WOULD YOU LOVE ME LIKE THAT?

When the essence of love is lost and confined to self

Would you love me like that?

When all that left of me is the narcissism and all I can do is take and never repay

Would you love me like that?

When all I can feel is hate for love and hate for the admirer

Would you love me like that?

When all I am is a self-criticized actuator

Would you love me like that?

When I fail to reject myself and reject you indeed

Would you love me like that?

When I treat a helping hand of affirmation as a
threat to my existence

Would you love me like that?

When I befriend the inanimate and seek
vengeance from the animate

Would you love me like that?

When I exempt myself from endearment and
convict myself of yearning

Would you love me like that?

Random Thoughts

I want to converse over the phone and cry
with you.
I want to dream with you.
Although we are miles away I want our
heartbeats to be in sync.
We might not talk, might not text, might not
have met but be with me! Be in sync!

I want to stare at you till you blush.
I want to hold you till you stop resisting.
I want to hug you till you drop your tears on
my shoulders.
I want to kiss you till you are out of breath.
And there's a don't I want from you, I don't
want to lose you till I count my last breath.

How shameless is she to say she's not a thief, my heart just missed a beat.

Although love's an abstract entity, there's this quest for "truth" in it.

The problem doesn't lie in the fact that you can't force someone to love you back but in the fact that you too cannot force yourself to love someone. Love blossoms from nowhere.

Everyone is someone's dream or nightmare.

Those smiles were not to be responded to,
loosing myself swiftly .
Those pair of eyes are so alluring it demands
to be followed,
it was never to be seen .
The melodious voice of her so seducing ,
they were never to be heard.
Her hypnotic touch leaves my blood rushing,
she was never to be touched.
The flux of her aroma so magnetic,
it was not to be smelt, her ignorance so
excruciating she was never to be witnessed.

If you have desires, you are alive.
If you are alive, you are bound to have
desires.
Else you are enlightened…

There's always something more he wants to know. Something that no one else does. He wants to breach her privacy, to which no one has access to. The desperate soul needs to hallucinate her soul with his aura and plague her forever with his taut love because there's always something more the soul wants to know.

Years will pass, memories will fade, panic will cease but whenever the heart will cry it will call you with all its might.

It is not the time that is wrong but your attitude that judges it.

You rendered me incomplete, breaking into pieces an art that would never be a masterpiece. A flawless art that my HEART was.

Love is a parasite that breeds on your feelings don't let it eat you from within.

Don't be proud on breaking my heart, it was intentional, really! I was just testing my resistance. I am an engineer and was just verifying OHM's law.

When life doesn't give you a chance, give life a chance and say "hey come on life, try once again I haven't given up yet" you will see one-day life will give all it has withheld.

Abstract is verbose.

There are days when we talk a lot and there are days we don't talk at all. There are days when I am happy and there are days I am not. There are days I feel victorious and there are days I feel I lost it all. I know I am with you as you want me to but you are not as I want you to be. I don't know when I crossed that line of friendship but remember I was a true friend to you once and can you not cross that line for me if you ever were a true friend to me.

Whatever you are up to please do it but don't ask me how I feel because you've never given happiness and therefore you can brag and grin about it but don't expect me to promote it for you -to destiny and life (wicked brothers).

The virtue which tends to falling in love is such that it opposes the cause if it is not reciprocated equally.

There was a time when I ruled every heart and mind and when you left, I donated it all to you selflessly. You took it away and never looked back making me a mere peasant in my own kingdom. That's the thing I earned after losing all to you.

Loving someone or falling for someone is the same. Initially you are after it and then love is after you to haunt and hunt.

She trespassed my vicinity, messed up with my belongings and left, making it vulnerable forever.

Nowadays no one talk s to me so I gossip with myself and notice that there are lot of noises inside me!

Every day I look at the moon and say why don't you get lost? The moon replies! I do once every month and then you beg me to come back because only I am common between you and her.

And it felt like forever… Add content to forever and not resentment because in the end forever was never yours only the content was!

The best thing about a dream is that even a blind person can have it.

Why there's a silence after every war? Why there's a silence after every quarrel? Why there's a silence after every accomplishment? Why there's a silence after every heartbreak? That's because silence holds answers to a lot of inexplicable questions.

Yesterday you had a heart but no love.

Today you have love but no heart to love.

Tomorrow you will have love and a heart but no heartbeat.

You never choose fate, fate chooses you, but destiny, you can choose.

Philosophies of the mind and profound fantasies of the heart is what love is comprised of.

Don't ask me what love is? If you can solve the mysteries behind quantum mechanics, well, then you would be somewhat as far as the sun.

Cheers and shouts are what you see

What I see is a silence within voices

And screams within silence.

My eyes know my secrets but it doesn't retain. My eyes resemble her now and I have shut myself with the memories I have. I no longer see the world as it is. It's just darkness but there's a precious jewel I have and that is her. Her world was dark but now it has two precious jewel that enlightens her soul. Her world has diversified colors because my eyes are not here and it resembles her now.

I wanted to give my all to her, but all for myself

But it was all for her

Because I wanted her to be happy and my happiness was in hers

But then it was my happiness that was in hers.

#selfish or love?

Rational people tend to change their oath according to the circumstances.

Irrational ones tend to play it on their principles.

The world relies on the permutation and combinations of philosophies.

Nevertheless, choice is your faith

And to keep faith is only your choice.

Thank You Note

There has been a long period of negligence and delay in compiling the emotions conveyed in this collection as I have been very erratic with my writings. Although the content is mine but the actual ideation of the book has been done by Abhisar Garg. He has been playing so many roles as and when the need be. Be it a motivator, a proof reader, the book designer, a publisher or a great friend. He has always been there and very patiently adhered to all my requests. So my first thanks are for you my friend.

To all my readers who read my first book and suggested me to keep writing and who are not physically there but are omnipresent on the digital platforms. Thank you guys for appreciating my work. I hope you all will love this too.

A very special thanks to J. Alchem Sir. He has been the best mentor I have come across. He has been guiding me on how to write good and efficiently. He has been a very good listener to all my nonsense and all supported me.

I cannot forget to mention Priyanka Bansal di, Akansh Malik, Priyanka Bose. They have been such lovely people that this mention is also too less a compliment for them.

Finally, very very thanks to all my lovely readers. You are the reason for this book.

LOVE STORY? SERIOUSLY!

The sanguine sun is just preparing to slumber and the filtered glare from it striking the scene makes it even more alluring. The flock of birds are moving together in a v shaped structure and it looks as if they are returning to their home after a long tedious day's hard work. The fact that they are all together in every aspect of life brings strength and calmness to my dilapidating heart. It is even more mesmerizing to find the three best people of my life beside me. SAMAR: The epitome of the story, takes you on an amazing voyage of his life. He recalls his friends and all his unsuccessful love interests - Sapna, Samriddhi and Surbhi. What happens when you fall in love? What happens when you fall out of it? What happens when you are unwanted? What happens when you are cheated and still coined a cheater? Can there be a reason to not like someone? Can there always be a reason to like someone? Explore answers to all these questions along with Samar on his journey in search of true love. It brings you, yet another unconventional love story of all times. The author intends to bring about the fact that can this also be a love story and leaves the readers to decide enquiring them Love Story? Seriously!

INKQUILLS's Other Books